Aliens
for
Breakfast

by Jonathan Etra
and Stephanie Spinner
illustrated by Steve Björkman

A STEPPING STONE BOOK™

Random House 🏠 New York

www.randomhouse.com/kids

Library of Congress Cataloging-in-Publication Data
Etra, Jonathan. Aliens for breakfast / by Jonathan Etra and Stephanie Spinner.
    p.   cm. — (A Stepping stone book)
SUMMARY: Finding an intergalactic special agent in his cereal box, Richard joins in a fight to save Earth from the Dranes, one of whom is masquerading as a student in Richard's class.
ISBN 0-394-82093-2 (pbk.) — ISBN 0-394-92093-7 (lib. bdg.)
[1. Extraterrestrial beings—Fiction. 2. Science fiction.] I. Spinner, Stephanie.
II. Title. PZ7.E854Al 1988 Fic—dc19 88-6653

Printed in the United States of America   51

To Mom—J.E.
To Calista—S.S.

1.

"Mom, I hate these sneakers." Richard Bickerstaff was getting dressed for school.

"You picked them out yourself last week, sweetie," his mother called from the kitchen.

"Last week they were okay. Today I hate them." Richard frowned at his feet. Why had he ever chosen these dumb black high-tops? He should have gotten red-leather running shoes like Dorf's. They were cool. But then, Dorf was cool. He had just moved here. He'd only been in Richard's class for two days, but already the other kids were imitating him.

They were copying his big smile, which showed off his perfect white teeth. And they were copying the way he dressed. On the first day he came to school, Dorf wore a red bowling shirt. It had his name, Dorf, spelled out on the pocket. The next day Richard's best friend, Henry, wore a bowling shirt. It had "Sylvia" stitched on the pocket. Everyone thought it was pretty great anyway.

Richard poked around in his closet, which was full of old Space Lords of Gygrax comics. He didn't have a bowling shirt and he knew it. But he looked anyway.

"Richard, finish dressing or you won't have time for breakfast," called his mother. "Hurry up. I have some new cereal for you to try."

Richard found a clean shirt and put it on. "I hate cereal," he said as he came into the kitchen. He scowled at his cereal bowl. It was full of strange little brightly colored shapes. "And this stuff is looking at me!" he added. All the strange little shapes had tiny silver eyes.

"It's called Alien Crisp," said his mother. She poured some milk into Richard's bowl. "I thought you'd like it, since you're such a sci-fi fan."

The little shapes seemed to grow as the milk touched them. Then everything in the bowl heaved and sighed.

Richard put down his spoon. "Mom, where did you find this stuff? It's alive!"

"Richard, your imagination is getting out of hand," said his mother. "It's a free sample. I found it in the mailbox."

"But it's moving!"

"The milk is making it move."

"The milk is standing still. The cereal is moving."

"Well, wait until it stops moving. Then eat it," said Mrs. Bickerstaff. "I have to get ready for work." Mrs. Bickerstaff was a lawyer. She almost never minded arguing. Except when she was in a hurry. Like now.

"I don't think it's cereal," muttered Richard as she hurried out of the kitchen. He picked up the cereal box. "Alien Crisp" it said on the front. "Crunchy, Munchy Aliens in a Box! Packed on the Planet Ganoob and Rushed Straight to You!"

Richard eyed his bowl. Everything in it had stopped moving. Then the milk gave a tiny splash. A round pink thing the color of chewed bubblegum started to climb up the side of the bowl. Amazed, Richard touched it with his spoon.

"Stop that!" The words came directly into Richard's head. He put his spoon down very quickly. Then he took off his glasses and wiped them on his shirt sleeve. But when he put them back on, the thing was still there.

"What do you think you're doing?" asked the voice.

"Uh, eating breakfast," answered Richard. Was a piece of cereal really talking to him?

It was. "I could use some breakfast myself," it said. It crawled out of the bowl and dropped onto the table. "The trip really took it out of me."

Richard finally found his voice. "Who are you?" he asked.

"Aric. Commander of the Interspace Brigade. Our goal: to wipe out cosmic troublemakers. Our record: ninety-eight percent success."

"You're an alien?" squeaked Richard. All those books he'd read about kids meeting aliens. And now it looked like it was happening to him. Him! Richard Bickerstaff!

"I am a Ganoobian," said Aric. *"You* are the alien."

I've got to be dreaming, thought Richard. He sometimes had very exciting dreams about space travel and large but friendly creatures from other planets who made him their leader.

"Well, come on! Do not just sit there!" said Aric. His voice was awfully loud for such a little thing. It boomed inside Richard's head. "Let us get going—I am busy. I have six other planets to save. Move it or lose it! Hup-hup-hup!"

"Wait a minute," said Richard. "Where are we going? Who are we fighting? What about school? I'm going to be late!"

"Hey—it is your planet," said Aric. "And you have been chosen to help me save it. But if you do not mind the Dranes taking over, hunky-dory." He started to climb back into Richard's cereal bowl.

"Who are the Dranes?" Richard wondered

if they were tiny and pink, like Aric.

"Space trash," said Aric. "Mean. Very mean. When the Dranes see a planet they like, they move in. Before the natives know it, their minds are mush. And the Dranes are in control. Forever!"

"And these, uh, Dranes. They're here?" asked Richard.

"Yes, they are here. Or to be precise, one is here. But one is more than enough. Dranes divide every four days. In a few weeks Earth will be knee-deep in them. Not a pretty sight."

"What does this Drane look like?" asked Richard.

"Well, Dranes can look like anything they want to. The one here has blond hair, blue eyes, and a smile no one can resist. He is in your class. He just showed up two days ago."

"Dorf? Dorf is an alien?" Richard was so excited he jumped out of his chair. He couldn't wait to tell Henry.

"My job is to get rid of the Drane before he divides," said Aric. Then, for a moment, he looked a little confused. "You have suitable weapons, of course."

"Weapons? All I've got is a water gun!" Somehow Richard knew that wouldn't be enough to stop a Drane.

Aric sat down on the table. "Maybe it is because I am not used to being soaked in milk," he said. "But I cannot remember—"

"You can't remember what?" asked Richard.

"The weapon to use against the Drane." Aric looked confused again.

"You mean you didn't bring weapons with you on your spaceship?"

"I have no ship," said the little alien.

"Then how did you get here?"

"I was freeze-dried and beamed from Ganoob in a cereal box. Fast and cheap," said Aric.

"Well, have them beam the right weapons down," said Richard.

"No, no—you do not understand," said Aric. "The weapon is here, on your planet. That is why I did not bring it. It is something found in many Earthling homes. Only, now—" He scratched his little pink head. "I cannot remember what it is!"

"Richard!" called Mrs. Bickerstaff. "School bus is here."

Richard scooped up his books and his lunchbox. "Look," he said. "I'm just a kid. And I have to go to school. You're the space warrior. You figure out what to do."

To Richard's surprise, Aric jumped onto his shoulder. "I am coming with you," he said. "Perhaps I will regain my memory when I see the Drane. Let us go forth!"

Richard plucked Aric off his shoulder. He tucked him gently into his shirt pocket. " 'Bye, Mom," he called. "I'm off to save the world."

"Have fun, sweetie," answered Mrs. Bickerstaff.

2.

Richard slid into his seat just as math was starting. He was under strict orders from Aric to act normal. "Do not let anyone know about me," he had told Richard on the way to school. "If the Drane finds out I am here, you can kiss this planet good-bye." So now Richard couldn't stare at Dorf, even though he wanted to. Instead he had to pretend that the only thing on his mind was the question Mrs. Marks was asking.

As usual, it was a hard one.

"Who knows how many ways we can make

change for a dollar?" she asked. She looked around the room slowly. Then she stared straight at Richard. His heart sank. "Richard?" she asked.

Richard knew you could get four quarters or ten dimes or a hundred pennies from a dollar. But that was too easy. This was a trick question with a trick answer. Only he didn't know the answer.

"Any ideas, Richard?" asked Mrs. Marks.

"Four?"

"Only four?"

"Five," he said quickly. He would have to bluff.

"Who thinks there are more?" asked Mrs. Marks.

"There must be at least ten," called Henry. He was good at trick questions. "What about a mixture of nickels, dimes, and pennies? Or nickels, quarters, and half-dollars?"

Half-dollars! thought Richard. I forgot those.

Then Dorf raised his hand. He had a big smile on his face. It showed off his perfect white teeth.

"Yes, Dorf?" said Mrs. Marks.

"There are two hundred ninety-two ways to change a dollar bill," said Dorf.

All the kids in the class stared at Dorf. How had he come up with that number?

"Good guess!" exclaimed Mrs. Marks.

"It's not a guess," said Dorf. "I figured it out last summer. On my computer."

"Well, you're very clever indeed," said Mrs. Marks. "Because that is the right answer. Can anyone explain why?" Her eyes moved up and down the rows. Richard tried to look invisible.

"You have pennies, nickels, dimes, quarters, and half-dollars," continued Dorf. "One hundred thirty-six coins in all. But you can mix them in all kinds of ways. Like five pennies, two dimes, five nickels, and a half-dollar. Or forty-five pennies, a nickel, and two quarters. There are hundreds of ways to do it. Two hundred ninety-two ways, to be exact," he finished smoothly.

Mrs. Marks didn't smile a lot. But she smiled now. And everyone in the class nodded, as if Dorf had just said something important and wonderful.

"He has begun to control their minds," said Aric. Richard jumped. For a moment he had forgotten about the alien in his pocket. Now he felt a thrill of alarm at Aric's words. What should he do?

"I told you before," said Aric's voice. "Just act normal. Do you understand?"

"Yes," said Richard silently, sensing that Aric could hear his thoughts. He felt hot and nervous. But at least math was over. He walked over to Henry's seat with his lunch box. They always traded sandwiches after math. Richard's mother made him tuna on whole wheat, which he hated. Henry's mother made him peanut butter and jelly, which *he* hated. So they traded. But when Richard got to Henry, Henry was already eating a sandwich. It looked like tuna fish. Dorf was sitting next to Henry. He was eating a sandwich, too. It looked like peanut butter and jelly.

"Hey!" said Richard. "Don't you want to trade?"

"Already have," said Henry, with his mouth full. "I traded with Dorf." His eyes, when he turned to Richard, looked funny. Almost as if they weren't focused right.

"But we always trade," said Richard.

"Here, Richard. Have half of mine," said Dorf. He offered his peanut butter and jelly with a smile.

"Do not look at his teeth." Aric's voice popped into Richard's mind. "They send out dangerous Drane rays that will bring you under his control. Look only into his eyes. They cannot harm you."

Richard took a deep breath and turned to Henry. "I hate tuna fish," he said. "And we always trade. How could you give my sandwich away?"

"It's not your sandwich. Anyway, Dorf got to me first," said Henry.

Richard sputtered with anger. "He's a—" Before he could say "Drane monster," Henry broke in.

"He's a great guy," said Henry. His mouth was still full of tuna fish. "He's got his own VCR and all the Mad Max tapes. And he's going to let me watch them on Saturday."

"Why don't you come too?" said Dorf. "A

whole bunch of kids from the class are coming. It'll be fun."

"I hate Mad Max!" said Richard, though this wasn't true. Then he saw that Henry was staring straight at Dorf. Right at Dorf's perfect smile. "And besides, I'm already busy," he finished weakly.

Then he sat down at his desk and looked blankly at his tuna sandwich. Earth is in BIG trouble, thought Richard Bickerstaff.

3.

All day Richard kept waiting for Aric to remember what the secret weapon was. But Aric didn't remember. Instead, he complained. He whined about having to stay in Richard's pocket. He made rude remarks about the classes he had to sit through. The only time he stopped complaining was during gym. Then he sat in the pocket of Richard's shorts and didn't make a sound. After gym he confessed that the smell of the basketball reminded him of Ingbar, his girlfriend on Ganoob.

But at last the school day was almost over.

Only art was left—Richard's favorite. He had been working for weeks on a drawing of the starship *Enterprise*. Now it was nearly finished. He settled down and got to work. Using a silver crayon, he drew in one last fin on the ship's side. "Isn't this great?" he asked Aric silently. Now that he knew he could send thoughts to the little alien, he was beginning to like it.

"Primitive," answered Aric. "Besides, interspace beaming is much cheaper."

"But what if you don't know exactly where you're going? Captain Kirk never has a destination. He spends his time on the *Enterprise* exploring space. Looking for strange new worlds."

"Get real. We have enough problems with the worlds we know already. Thanks to our friends the Dranes. In case you had forgotten."

Richard threw down his crayon. "How could I forget?" he said out loud. Too late, he remembered about sending the thought silently. What if someone in class heard him talking to himself? They would think he was crazy.

But no one even looked at him. His whole class was watching in silence as Dorf worked on his art project. Richard wondered why everyone was so impressed. After all, it was only a little white paper pyramid.

Mrs. Logan walked over to Dorf's desk. Dorf smiled one of his big smiles up at her. Her eyes got a little funny and glassy as she smiled back. "How beautiful!" she said to Dorf. "So three-dimensional!"

Henry was sitting next to Dorf. He stared at Dorf's pyramid for a long time. Then he stared at his own crayon drawing of two dinosaurs. Then he looked back at Dorf's pyramid again.

"Mrs. Logan, can I make something new?" he asked.

"What would you like to make, Henry?" asked Mrs. Logan.

"Uh, something three-dimensional. Like Dorf."

"What a nice idea!" said Mrs. Logan. "Of course! Go ahead."

Then Celia raised her hand. She was drawing a picture of dancing jellybeans. "Me, too," she said.

"Me, too," said Jennifer, Ruth, Philip, George, Leroy, Fawn, Dawn, Sean, and Tristram. Mrs. Logan looked pleased.

"If you'd all like to try something new, go right ahead," she said. The whole class got up. They walked to the supply table and took what was left of the white paper. Then they walked back to their seats and began making little white pyramids. They look like a bunch of robots, thought Richard.

Mrs. Logan came over to him. "Is something wrong?" she asked. "Don't you want to try something new too?"

"Not really," said Richard. "I haven't finished my starship yet."

Suddenly Mrs. Logan leaned closer. "What's that on your hand?" she asked. "Are you bleeding?"

Richard looked at his fingers. Yikes! The tips were bright red. Blood was oozing out from under his fingernails.

Richard grabbed his hand. "How did this happen? I didn't cut myself. I'm sure of it." Out of the corner of his eye he saw Dorf smile. Why?

"Do not look at his teeth," Aric told him. "Get out of class."

"You'd better go to the nurse," said Mrs. Logan. "She'll take care of you."

Richard stood, holding his hand up stiffly. Henry tore his eyes away from his pyramid. "Does it hurt?" he asked.

"Naw," said Richard, as if it were no big deal. The truth was, it didn't hurt. But it scared him. He knew he hadn't cut himself. Or had he?

"You did not," Aric told him on the way to the nurse's office. "I am sorry to have to break this to you. Dorf knows you are resisting him. So he is pulling a cheap Drane trick. He is rearranging your molecules. You are melting."

Richard stopped in his tracks. "Melting!"

"Well, dissolving is more like it," said Aric. "Your molecules are drifting apart. Slowly, of course."

They were outside the nurse's office. "This is terrible!" moaned Richard. How had he ever thought getting to know an alien would be fun? He felt like throwing up.

"It will not get much worse today or tomorrow," said Aric. "But I hope you do not have big plans for the weekend."

Richard whimpered.

"Once I remember the secret weapon, I can destroy Dorf. Then you will be fine," said Aric.

"But what if you *don't* remember?"

"If I do not remember," said Aric, "Earth will be so deep in Dranes that dissolving will be fun."

4.

Back in his own room after school, Richard looked at his bandaged fingers and tried to fight his panic. It wasn't easy. The fact that his fingertips had started to ache made it even harder. He thought of Dorf and shuddered.

"Listen, Aric," he said as calmly as he could. "Don't you think we should do some serious thinking about how to get Dorf? I mean, are you sure you don't have some superpowerful weapon stashed away? How about a sub-ion warp disrupter?" That was what the Space Lords of Gygrax used to blow away *their* enemies. It always worked. At least in the comics.

Aric jumped down off the stack of Yoda comics on Richard's shelf. He came to rest on the shoulders of a plastic King Kong. "Fancy weapons are too expensive for us,

Richard," he said. "The Interspace Brigade works on a very tight budget. We have 47 million planets to look after. Our yearly allowance is 249 billion daktils. That comes to about sixty-seven cents a planet."

"Sixty-seven cents to save Earth?" shouted Richard. "That's it?"

"That is plenty," said Aric. "We saved Zweeb for thirty-six cents two years ago. Dranes are a cheap menace. They can be fought with simple ingredients."

"Like WHAT??" yelled Richard.

"It will come to me," said Aric. "Just give me time."

"I can't believe it," said Richard. "My planet is being taken over by space hoodlums. I'm melting. And you, the *commander* of the Interspace Brigade, can't remember a simple ingredient!" His toes began to throb. Were they bleeding, like his fingers? He was too scared to take off his high-tops and look.

"I never said I was perfect!" snapped Aric. He slipped down off King Kong and started pacing. Then he stopped.

"Perhaps I could look around your house.

It might bring back my memory," he said.

"Sure. Where do you want to start? Garage? Kitchen? Bathroom?"

"I seem to remember that the substance can be eaten," said Aric. "Where do you store items of nourishment?"

"In the kitchen!" cried Richard. He grabbed Aric and headed down the hall.

Ten minutes later the Bickerstaff kitchen looked like a supermarket after an earthquake. The floor was covered with the contents of the refrigerator. Now Richard was emptying all the shelves. As he did, he showed each item to Aric. "This is peanut butter. This is hot chocolate. This is rice. These are graham crackers. These are pickles. These are soft drinks—Tab for Mom, Dr Pepper for me. Salt. Sugar. Tuna. See anything that will kill a Drane?"

"I do not think so," said Aric. He was sitting on a bunch of grapes. "And I really thought I would remember it right away."

"Dorf hasn't clouded your mind, has he?" asked Richard.

"This is an easy mission," said Aric. "I have

wiped out Dranes on lots of other planets.
Though I have never been freeze-dried be-
fore. It must have shaken me up." He sighed.
"We had better keep looking."

Richard got back to work. "How about
these?" he asked. "Chocolate sprinkles for ice
cream."

"Afraid not," said Aric. "Is this all?" The floor, the counters, the kitchen table and chairs were now covered with bottles, boxes, cans, and jars of food.

"Yes," said Richard.

"It is not here," said the alien. "Perhaps we

can search some other Earthling's home? One with a wider range of products?"

"We have the best kitchen on the planet," said Richard. "Mom buys everything. If it isn't here, I don't know where it could be." Then he had an idea. "Unless you want to go to the mall."

"Is there food at the mall?"

"Every fast food made in America."

"Then by all means let us go there," said Aric. "And quickly!"

5.

The mall was busy for a Thursday afternoon. Richard wondered why. Then he saw that one of the stores was having a promotion. It was for a new men's perfume called Sweat. A big fat man dressed like a wrestler was giving out free samples.

"Ugh! Why would anyone want to buy that stuff?" said Richard.

"To attract the female of the species, of course," said Aric.

"Girls? I can see spending money to keep them *away*," said Richard. "But I'd rather spend it on something cool. Like that." He pointed at a black satin baseball jacket in the window of a store. "I don't have enough money, though. Mom says maybe she'll get it for my next birthday. . . . Of course, I may never *have* another birthday." Richard's hands and feet were really hurting now.

"After we have destroyed the Drane, the Brigade may find some extra money to buy you a gift," said Aric. "You have earned something for all you have been through."

Aric sounded so sure of destroying Dorf that Richard felt a little better. "Gee, thanks—"

he started to say. But Aric interrupted him. "Great Ganoob!" cried the alien. "What is that?"

They were next to Mutant Splendor, a store that sold sci-fi games, books, toys, masks, and comics. It was just about Richard's favorite place in the whole world. Today the front of the store was taken up by a giant display of the Space Lords of Gygrax. The big plastic warriors had bright red wings, blue skin, and webbed feet. They were all snarling and holding laser swords, as if they were about to

attack. The display had sound effects, too—battle noises and strange space music.

Richard's mouth dropped open. For a second he forgot that his hands and feet hurt. This was awesome! Ten times better than the comic books!

But Aric didn't think so. "You call these Gygraxians?" he snapped. "They are a joke!"

"You mean there really is a planet Gygrax?" asked Richard.

"Of course," said Aric. "But Gygraxians do not have wings. They have fins. Not only that, their skin is orange, not blue. And they never fight. They are the biggest cowards in the galaxy. This is an outrage! I want to speak to the manager."

Aric started to hop out of Richard's pocket. Richard clamped a hand around him. "How can you get so upset about a bunch of stupid toys? Time is running out! You have to remember what the secret weapon is!" Was it Richard's imagination? Or was he beginning to feel wobbly? Maybe he was dissolving faster!

"Aric—" Richard went on. But then he froze.

Dorf and Henry were walking down the mall. They were dressed in the same red T-shirts and ripped jeans. Dorf was talking, and Henry was listening. He nodded his head at everything Dorf said. As Richard watched, they walked into Pizza World.

"Aric!" gasped Richard. "There they are! Dorf and Henry! Should we follow them, or what?"

"Follow," answered Aric.

"I've never trailed anybody before. What if they see us?"

"Do not worry," said Aric. "I will make us invisible."

"What! You can do that? How come you didn't do it before?"

"It is very expensive. Only for emergencies," said Aric. "And it only lasts ten minutes. Now let us go." He made a low humming sound that filled Richard's head for a moment. As he crossed over to Pizza World, Richard found himself humming too. He couldn't help himself.

When he reached for the door of the pizza parlor, Richard's hand disappeared. He looked down at his feet. They weren't there either. He was invisible!

6.

Being invisible was a little scary. Richard couldn't see or feel himself. So he couldn't tell where he began or ended. As he walked into Pizza World, he moved his arms and legs very slowly. He was hoping he wouldn't bump into anything. But even though he was really careful, he did. When he passed a table of four teenaged girls, he knocked over all their empty soda cups. Ice cubes and paper cups went flying. The girls screamed. Richard froze.

"Keep going!" Aric's voice boomed inside

Richard's head. "Have you never been invisible before?"

"Are you kidding?" answered Richard. "I'm human. We can't do that."

Aric gave a tiny snort. "Well, then," he said, "just sit down quietly. Try not to move around a lot. At least no one knows that we are here. The Drane is too busy with his food."

Dorf and Henry were sitting at a table covered with pizza pies and soft drinks. Richard held his breath. Then he sat down quietly beside Henry. It looked to Richard as if the pizzas were the house special—Death by Pizza. They had peas, carrots, onions, cheese, and wheat germ on them. Death by Pizzas were famous on the mall. No one had ever died from eating one. But people had come close.

"Just before Dranes divide they build up their power by eating a lot," said Aric. Richard's heart sank. There were seven pizzas on the table.

"Hey, these look really good!" Dorf licked his lips. "And isn't it great being here without that little nerd Richard?"

"Yeah. It's great, Dorf," said Henry in a spaced-out voice.

Richard felt like giving Dorf an invisible punch. "Maybe Dorf will die from the pizza," he said to Aric.

"No," said Aric. "The pizza will simply help him to divide faster."

Dorf picked up a glass shaker of red-hot pepper flakes and poured it all on one of the pizzas. He breathed in clouds of red dust. A big smile broke out over his face. Then he reached over to an empty table and grabbed another glass shaker. He poured pepper flakes over a second pizza.

Suddenly Dorf sprang up. He went from table to table, picking up all the pepper shakers. When his arms were full, he came back and sat down. He lined all the shakers up in front of him. Henry looked puzzled.

"What are you doing, Dorf?" he asked.

"Eating!" Dorf turned his widest smile on Henry. "I'm hungrier than I thought." One by one, he emptied all the shakers onto the pizzas. Henry gulped and turned green.

"What is in the bottles?" Aric asked Richard.

"Red-hot pepper flakes. The hottest stuff in the world. I can't believe he can eat all that and not explode."

"That is it!" shouted Aric. "Red pepper! I knew I would remember! That is the weapon!"

"Great!" Richard watched Dorf closely. He could hardly wait to see what the pepper flakes would do. But nothing happened. Dorf wasn't dying. He wasn't even looking sick. He was enjoying himself! He devoured slice after slice of the pizza, eating faster and faster.

Henry nibbled on the edge of a piece. Then he ran gasping for water. Dorf paid no attention. He ate and ate. His fair skin turned pink. His blue eyes flashed purple. A terrible greedy smile spread over his face, which was now covered with cheese and bits of carrot.

"How come it's not working, Aric?" asked Richard. "I mean, if it's the weapon, shouldn't he be getting weak or something?" Then Richard had an awful thought. What if Aric was wrong? What if the pepper flakes didn't work against Dorf?

"I am not wrong!" snapped Aric. Too late, Richard remembered that Aric could hear his thoughts. "It is all coming back to me now. The weapon is pepper flakes. Dranes cannot resist it. Once they start eating it they cannot stop. And then they explode."

"Then how come he's so happy?" asked Richard. If anything, Dorf looked stronger now than before.

"If he were eating just pepper flakes, he would indeed die soon," said Aric. "But he is eating pizza also. And that is giving him strength."

"What can we do?" asked Richard.

"We must feed him pepper flakes. And only pepper flakes," said Aric. "Enough to destroy him. And we must work quickly."

"Okay, I'll give it to him," said Richard. "Tomorrow. At school."

"Very good," said Aric.

By the time Henry came back, Dorf was on his last pizza. His face was bright red. Henry was staring into his empty cup. He looked sick.

"I don't feel so good," he said.

"Have another slice," said Dorf.

"Could we go home now? I think I'd better lie down."

"I'm almost finished. I feel really great. There's nothing like a pizza to get your blood flowing!" shouted Dorf. "How about running around the mall a few times?"

"Maybe later," mumbled Henry. Then he jumped up and ran off to the bathroom.

"We had better go," said Aric. "We are going to become visible again in about a minute."

Richard got up. Very carefully he made his way around the chairs and tables. He opened the front door and slid out of Pizza World. Then he headed back to Mutant Splendor. No one would notice if a kid and a tiny alien materialized there. They'd think it was some new game or promotion or something. And that was exactly what happened.

7.

The next morning Richard was up early. "Well, I guess today we save the universe," he said nervously. Aric was curled up in an orange Frisbee. He yawned and stretched.

"It is not the universe. Just your little home planet," he answered.

"I resent that," said Richard. He pulled his socks on over his bandaged feet. "If it's so small and unimportant, why are you here?" Richard's head was pounding. Was that part of melting too? In any case he was sick of Aric acting like such a know-it-all.

"All right. All right. Your planet *is* important. If the Dranes take over Earth, who knows what they will do next? But it is bad luck to brag, and worse manners. Your mother should have taught you that."

"She tried," said Richard. He went into his closet and pulled out a five-pound box of pepper flakes. He felt so weak that it was hard to lift the box. And he had spent $17.52 on it—his life savings.

"I sure hope this works," he said. "Do you think five pounds is enough?"

"It better be. Dorf will divide in exactly three hours and fourteen minutes. Then it is bye-bye, biosphere."

Richard shuddered. "I guess we'd better hurry," he said. "There's no place else to go if we mess up, is there?"

"Negatory, my friend," said Aric.

"Richard!" called Mrs. Bickerstaff. "Time to get up!"

Richard put Aric into his shirt pocket. He zipped the box of pepper flakes into his backpack. Then he walked into the kitchen. His mother, in her bathrobe, was opening and closing all the cabinets. "Where did the tea bags go?" she said. "I could swear they were in here yesterday."

"Gee, Mom, I sure don't know," said Richard. He and Aric had cleaned up the kitchen the afternoon before in a big hurry. They probably should have been more careful.

"You're up early this morning," said his mother. "How come? Something special going on at school?"

"No. Just felt like getting an early start," said Richard.

"Good for you! What would you like for breakfast? Some more of that nice new cereal?"

"No!" Richard croaked. He never wanted to see another box of Alien Crisp in his life.

Richard's mother peered at him. "Are you all right, honey?" she asked. "You look pale."

For a second Richard felt like a little kid again. He wished he could tell his mother everything. "I'm fine, Mom," he said. He sat down at the table. "Really."

"Well, at least have a good breakfast," said his mother. She smoothed back his hair. "How about an egg?"

"Sure," said Richard. To his mother's surprise he ate everything on his plate. Then he kissed her on the cheek and left to wait for the school bus right on time.

Richard was glad Henry wasn't on the bus. If he saw Henry, he wasn't sure he could keep quiet about Dorf. And he knew that saying anything would ruin Aric's mission. Then again, it was pretty clear that Henry was under Dorf's control. "He probably wouldn't believe me if I did tell him," thought Richard.

He walked into school and stood near the boys' bathroom. A second later Dorf and Henry came walking down the hall. They were both wearing red cowboy shirts and string ties. Dorf was talking, and Henry was nodding at everything he said. As usual.

"Remember. Do not look at Dorf's teeth when he smiles," said Aric. "And step back after you give him the flakes. Dranes can get violent before they explode."

Richard got hot. Then cold. Then slightly dizzy.

"Do not be afraid," said Aric.

"I'm not afraid. I'm terrified," said Richard. But even as he said it, he was stepping away from the wall. He stood in front of Dorf and Henry. "Hi, you guys," he said.

"Hi, Richard," said Dorf. "How are you doing? You don't look so good, buddy." Then he smiled one of his amazing smiles right at Richard. Just in time Richard remembered to look away. Then he said, "I was hoping I'd run into you before class, Dorf. I've got something I think you'll *really* like. Come on in here. I'll show it to you." He led them into the boys' bathroom, which was empty. Then he set his backpack down. It took all his strength to pull out the box of pepper flakes.

"Here. This is for you," Richard told Dorf. He opened the box. "Want some?"

Dorf looked at the pepper flakes. Suddenly his face was wet with sweat. He smiled a hungry smile. His breath came fast and hard, and his eyes gleamed. His face turned bright pink. He grabbed the box away from Richard. Then he poured a heap of pepper flakes into his hand. He stuffed it into his mouth as if he were eating popcorn. Only he didn't chew it. He simply swallowed it. Then he swallowed another handful. And another.

"Dorf! What are you doing?" cried Henry.

Dorf ignored him. His eyes turned bright purple. "More!" he gasped. He poured pepper flakes down his throat. "More!" The snaps on his cowboy shirt popped open. His chest was bright red. It started to steam. Henry jumped away. So did Richard. Now Dorf's eyes were bulging. He finished off the box and his skin went from red to purple. Then his hair started burning. It smelled horrible.

"Yikes!" said Richard. He grabbed Henry. They backed away toward the door.

Dorf began bubbling and popping. His clothes fell to the floor in a smoking heap. He stopped looking like a boy and started to look like a blob of live Silly Putty. Then he sprouted tentacles. There were dozens of them. They thrashed on the floor, making a loud hissing noise.

Richard felt something on his neck. He jumped. It was only Aric. He had climbed on Richard's shoulder to watch.

A horrible cry filled the bathroom. "You got me!" screamed Dorf. "Two more hours, and I would have started dividing. My clones would

have been all over your planet like ants on a candy bar! And then all you pathetic Earthlings would have been our slaves!" His tentacles flopped on the white floor.

"I hate to lose!" Dorf wailed at Richard. "I hope you flunk math and history. I hope you fail science and art and social studies and English and gym!"

Then he blew up.

8.

It had been a great day. Dorf was gone. Earth was saved. Richard had stopped melting. And he and Henry were friends again. In fact, now that Dorf was gone, everyone in Richard's class seemed a little friendlier. Richard didn't know why. It sure wasn't because anyone knew he'd saved the world.

The amazing thing was that no one even remembered Dorf anymore. Except for Henry. He was coming over later to spend the night. Richard planned to tell him all about the Dranes then.

The only bad thing about the day was that Aric was leaving.

"Can't you stick around for a while and hang out at the mall?" asked Richard. School was over, and he and Aric were back home. In a few minutes the Interspace Brigade was going to beam Aric back to Ganoob. He was leaving from the same place where he had landed—the Bickerstaff kitchen table.

"Sorry, the universe calls. Those Dranes never sleep," said Aric. "By the way, if you ever want to join the Brigade, just let me know."

"Would I get to fly around at light speed and blast monsters?" asked Richard. "Or wear a shiny red-and-blue uniform?"

"Mostly you have to travel fourth class in things like cereal boxes. And they make you wear baggy overalls, to blend in," sighed Aric.

"Oh," said Richard. That sounded almost as bad as school.

"The work is okay, though," added Aric. "Every now and then you run into a really brave freedom fighter. Someone who risks his life to save the world. That is truly satisfying."

It sounded like Aric was paying him a compliment. But Richard wasn't sure. "You mean me?" he asked.

"Absolutely."

"Wow. Thanks." He blushed. Then he asked, "Will I ever see you again?"

"Usually we do not go to a planet unless it is under attack," said Aric. "But sometimes we can work in a short stopover."

"That would be great! We could go to Mutant Splendor. And Pizza World. Just like old times."

"I would like that," said Aric. "And if you are ever near Ganoob, drop in. You would love Ingbar. Even if she is a girl Ganoobian."

Richard's heart sank. He knew he could never visit Ganoob. It was hard enough visiting his grandmother in California. But he managed to smile. "Sounds good. I'll try. Meanwhile, maybe you could send me a postcard sometime?"

"Maybe. Or maybe I will send you something else." By now Aric was standing on the salt shaker waiting for the Ganoobian transport beam. Suddenly he began to fade like a TV picture in a thunderstorm. "Goodbye,

Richard. Thank you." He waved.

" 'Bye, Aric. I'll miss you," said Richard. Then the alien was gone, and Richard started to cry.

The next morning Richard woke up suddenly. He sat up and rubbed his eyes. Henry opened his eyes at the same moment. He sat up too.

"Wow, Richard," he said. "I just had the most amazing dream. I don't know if it was all that stuff you told me about Aric, or what. But I dreamed I saw all these funny little pink creatures. They were bouncing up and down together in a big circle."

"Me too!" said Richard. "I had the same dream! Did you see two of them, sort of floating in the middle of the circle? Looking really, *really* happy?"

"Yeah. I wonder what was going on?" Henry yawned and got out of bed. He started to get dressed just as Mrs. Bickerstaff knocked on the door. "Rise and shine, boys!" she called. "Time to get up."

"I bet I know," said Richard. "I think it was

Aric's homecoming. And that was Ingbar with him in the circle." He smiled. "They sure looked like they were having a great time."

Richard opened his closet door. There on the floor was a brand-new black satin baseball jacket. On its back, in big gold letters, were the words "Interspace Brigade."

Richard picked it up and put it on. It was *really* cool. There was a note in one of the pockets.

"Thanks again," it said. "Wear this and have a pizza for me! See you, Aric."

About the Authors

JONATHAN ETRA was a humorist, playwright, and journalist, as well as a children's book author. He lived in New York City until his untimely death in 1991.

STEPHANIE SPINNER is a children's book editor and writer. She lives in New York City and has always wanted to go to Ganoob.

About the Illustrator

STEVE BJÖRKMAN is an illustrator whose work often appears in magazines. He notes, "I have been drawing ever since I was a kid. I was often reprimanded for doodling in class and now find it a great relief to do a drawing without having to hide it from the teacher." Steve Björkman lives in Irvine, California.

Leave room for...

the entire
Aliens trilogy!